For my forever loving Mum, Navigator of the Skies Dad and Dancing Queen sister Sara.
And for all little birds between two homes.

First published in 2016 by Child's Play (International) Ltd
Ashworth Road, Bridgemead, Swindon SN5 7YD, UK

Published in USA by Child's Play Inc
250 Minot Avenue, Auburn, Maine 04210

Distributed in Australia by Child's Play Australia Pty Ltd
Unit 10/20 Narabang Way, Belrose, Sydney, NSW 2085

Text and illustrations copyright © 2016 Jo Empson
The moral right of the author/illustrator has been asserted

ISBN 978-1-84643-889-9
CLP090915CPL11158899

Printed in Shenzhen, China

A catalogue record of this book
is available from the British Library

www.childs-play.com

Little Home Bird

by Jo Empson

Little Bird
loved his home.

Each day, he sat
on his favorite branch.

He ate his
favorite food.

He listened to
his favorite music.

And he looked out over his favorite view.
"Ahh," thought Little Bird, "HOME!"

But one day the wind blew cold
and the leaves started to fall.
Little Bird's big brother wrapped
his wing around him.

"Little Bird," he said. "Did you know a home can be here or there?
It may be near or far, big or small, and even hot or cold.
And sometimes you can have two homes — just like us!
It's time to fly south to our winter home,
where the food is plenty and
the wind's breath is warm."

Little Bird felt sad at
the thought of leaving his home.

He would miss sitting on his favorite branch,
eating his favorite food, listening
to his favorite music, and looking
out over his favorite view.

But then

he had

a good idea!

He would take all his favorite things with him.

Then, wherever he was, it would always feel like home!

All the birds gathered and their long journey began.

higher...

Higher...

...and higher
the birds flew.

And Little Bird followed with all his favorite things.

Little Bird tried to follow close to
the other birds' tails for fear of getting lost.
But soon he had to lessen his heavy load.

So with a splish and a splash...

...his favorite branch found a new home.

Much to a dog's delight!

And further south the birds flew.

The strong east wind blew and swept Little Bird on his way.

So with a whoosh

and a swoosh...

...his favorite music found a new home,
much to a shepherd's delight!

And further south
the birds flew.

The clouds clapped with a thunderous roar and sent Little Bird into a spin!

So with a rumble and a tumble...

...his favorite food found a new home,
much to a porcupine's delight!

And further south the birds flew.

After many days and many nights,
the birds reached their winter home
in the south, where the food was plenty
and the wind's breath was warm.

Little Bird no longer
had his favorite things.

But he discovered lots
of NEW favorite things!

And it soon felt like

HOME!

So twice each year, along with many other little birds,

Little Bird and his family would make

the long journey between their two homes.

Across oceans they would fly, over mountains

and through deserts — with many adventures along the way!